Silly Cat

An easy read picture book for kids

By Beth Hammond

Silly Cats
By Beth Hammond
ISBN-13: 978-1534723344
ISBN-10: 153472334X
Copyright 2016 Beth Hammond

For those who love to read, laugh, and above all love cats.

Fat Cat.

Thin cat.

Cat takes a nap.

Mad cat.

Wild cat.

Cat in a hat.

This cat sits beside a rose.

This cat has a tiny nose.

This cat really loves that dog.

This cat likes to play with frogs.

Orange cat.

Black cat.

Cat wants to play.

Fancy cat.

Alley cat.

Cat in the hay.

This cat caught a little mouse.

This cat sits inside a house.

This cat hides behind a branch.

This cat looks like he can dance.

Two cats.

Three cats.

Cat in a bag.

Fast cat.

Loud cat.

Cat looks sad.

This cat's sitting on a couch.

This cat really likes to pounce.

This cat's eyes are very bright.

This cat wants to say good night.

The End

If you enjoyed this book consider leaving an honest review!

Visit me at bethhammondbooks.com for more books in the Silly Easy Reads series.

Contact me at bethhammond@bethhammondbooks.com with any questions.

I love to hear from my readers. Thank you! - Beth

Made in United States
North Haven, CT
23 March 2022